What's in the River?

Written by Janeen Brian
Illustrated by Janine Dawson

An easy-to-read SOLO
for beginning readers

SOLOS

Southwood Books Limited
3-5 Islington High Street
London N1 9LQ

First published in Australia by Omnibus Books 2001

This edition published in the UK under licence from
Omnibus Books by
Southwood Books Limited, 2004

Text copyright © Amanda Graham 2001
Ilustrations copyright © Janine Dawson 2001

Cover design by Lyn Mitchell

ISBN 1 903207 75 4

Printed in China

A CIP catalogue record for this book is available
from the British Library

To Maggy,
a dear friend and conservationist – J.B.

To Rosie,
and all kids who love to read – J.D.

Chapter 1

Deep in the jungle was a great, green river. It was where all the animals and birds met. They chatted. They drank. They swam.

One day something strange happened.

Hippo was paddling under water. Paddle, paddle, paddle. She liked to hold her breath and count.

She had counted all the way to fifty and was about to burst.

Whoosh! Up she came.

CLUNK!

"Ouch!" cried Hippo. Something had hit her head. It made a lump. "What was that?" she asked.

There, by the edge of the river, was an odd-looking thing. Hippo pushed it up onto the river bank.

"What's that?" squawked Parrot.
"I don't know," said Hippo. She
felt the lump on her head. "I don't
know at all."

"Can you eat it?" asked Parrot.
She tried. She spat.

"Not much use then, is it?" she said, and flew off.

The odd-looking thing stayed where it was on the river bank.

Chapter 2

Next morning, Monkey was jumping all over the place.

Giraffe knew what Monkey wanted. It was what Monkey *always* wanted when Giraffe was around.

"All right," said Giraffe. "But only once. I don't want a sore neck."

Monkey climbed onto her back. "Ready! Steady! Go!" he shouted.

And he slid all the way down
Giraffe's neck and into the river.

"Wheee!" cried Monkey. Then,
"Ouch!"

Monkey had landed on something. He rubbed his bottom. "What was that?" he said.

It was another odd-looking thing.
This time it was sitting on the mud at
the bottom of the river.

Monkey rolled it up onto the bank.

"What's that?" squawked Parrot.
"I don't know," said Monkey. He
looked to see if he had a bump on
his bottom. "I don't know at all."

"Can you eat it?" asked Parrot. She tried. She spat.

"Not much use then, is it?" she said, and flew off.

The two odd-looking things sat on the river bank together.

Chapter 3

Next morning, Elephant waded into the river. He did his exercises. The exercise Elephant liked most was water-splashing.

Elephant sucked in a lot of water.

He blew it out again. He liked to make the water fly a long way!

Elephant sucked, and blew. The stream of water hit the river bank.

Elephant closed his eyes. He sucked hard. This time he would make the water go even further!

SPLAT!

"Ohh!" Elephant had sucked something into his trunk. It was stuck!

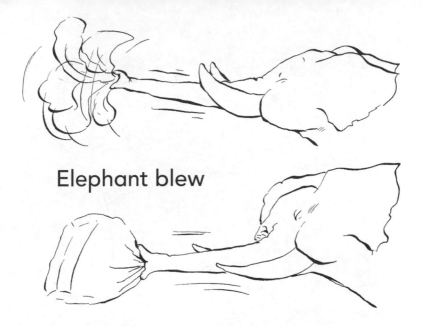

Elephant blew

... and blew ... and blew!

The something shot into the air.
It landed on the river bank.

"What's that?" squawked Parrot.
"I don't know," said Elephant.
He rested his sore trunk. "I don't
know at all."

"Can you eat it?" asked Parrot.
She tried. She spat.

"Not much use then, is it?" she
said, and flew off.

Chapter 4

The three things sat on the river bank together. What were they?

Hippo shook her head. "What can we do with them?" she said. "We don't know what they are."

"Well, you can't eat – " began
Parrot.
"We know that!" cried the others.

Giraffe wanted to know something else. "*Why* were they in the river?"

No one had an answer.

"They look very special," said
Monkey.
"Someone must have lost them,"
said Elephant.

Night fell. Still no one knew what the things were, or what to do with them.

And no one knew what to do
with the next thing. Or the next.
Or the next!

The pile grew and grew and
GREW!

Chapter 5

There was another problem. The things were in the way. The animals and birds liked their river bank the way it used to be.

What will we do? What *can* we do? What *should* we do? Questions buzzed around and around.

One day Giraffe called everybody together.

"I've been on a visit to my cousin," said Giraffe. "She said ..."

"Yes," said everybody, moving closer.

"She said those things aren't from the river at all. These are *not* river things."

Elephant waved his trunk. "If they are not river things," he said slowly, "what are they?"

Giraffe dipped her neck low. She rolled her eyes. She said, "They are *people* things!"

There was a gasp. Everybody stared at Giraffe.

"*People* things?" said Hippo. Her eyes squinted. "But there are no people in this jungle."

"Oh yes there are," said Giraffe. "There are people on the river bank, just past where the river bends. My cousin told me."

"But if that's true," said Elephant, "if these things *do* belong to people, why did we find them in the river?"

"Ah," said Giraffe. "That's the puzzle." She spoke softly. "My cousin thinks something bad might have happened at the people place. Something *terrible*."

"And did that make all their things fall in the river?" asked Monkey.

"Perhaps," said Giraffe.

For a moment everybody was quiet.

Then Hippo said, "That's sad. They must miss all their special things."

"It *is* sad," agreed the others.

Parrot flapped her wings. She flew onto Giraffe's head.

"I know," she said. "I know what we should do."

Everybody looked at Parrot. She told them her plan.

Chapter 6

It was a good plan. Everybody said so. But it wasn't easy.

It was hard to load the pile of things. It was hard to move the pile. And it was a long trip up the river.

By the time the jungle creatures reached the people place, all was dark and quiet.

Bit by bit, they unpacked the load and laid it down in neat piles.

When that was done, the jungle creatures smiled. They were tired, but they were happy.

It was time to go home.

"Won't the people get a surprise?" whispered Hippo.

"Yes," said Giraffe. "When they wake up, they'll see that everything has come back."

"All their *special* things," said Elephant.

And with that, Monkey jumped
onto Elephant's trunk.

Parrot flew onto Giraffe's head.

And Hippo led the way home, along the great, green river, deep in the jungle.

Janeen Brian

I have always loved birds and animals, trees, the sea and rivers. When I was little, I liked to paddle in streams.

These days, lots of our streams are dirty and full of rubbish. On special Clean-Up days, I help to clean them up. Sometimes I help clean up a river near where I live. I feel sad when I see all the rubbish. And I feel sad for the pelicans, ducks and other creatures who have to live among it. They need us to help them.

In *What's in the River?* I wrote about some animals who did *their* best to help *people.*

Janine Dawson

Many years ago, in the school holidays, my friend and I went to swim at a water hole. The water was deep and green and still. I was too scared to let my feet touch the bottom. Maybe some monster would slither over my toes!

When at last I did feel brave enough to touch the bottom, it didn't feel the way I thought it would. I was standing on something very strange. I lifted it out of the water, and saw that it was a set of false teeth!

I spent the rest of the day playing on the bank.

More Solos!

Duck Down
Janeen Brian and Michael Johnson

The Monster Fish
Colin Theale and Craig Smith

The Sea Dog
Penny Matthews and Andrew Mclean

Elephant's Lunch
Kate Darling and Mitch Vane

Hot Stuff
Margaret Clark and Tom Jellett

Spike
Phil Cummings and David Cox

Lily and the Wizard Wackoo
Judy Fitzpatrick and Don Hatcher

Sticky Stuff
Kate Walker and Craig Smith